Welcome to Speedway in May,
Where we all will have a wonderful
day.

**Cars traveled for miles down the interstate,
Traffic will be jam packed so be prepared to wait.**

The view from the sky looks so
amazing,
I can't wait to partake in the
celebration.

So many rabbits covered the track,
but it was time to race so they had to go
back.

Carb Day Concert had the westside rockin,
Once the music was on, there was no stopping.

**We loved every single minute of the parade,
It didn't even matter that our section had no shade.**

Fans grabbed their phones and took pics,
Race weekend in Indy is always so lit.

The taste of Mary Mom Unsers
amazing chili made you smile,
The mother of Indy 500 drivers
Bobby and Al.

Pork Tenderloin is a Race weekend fav,
Be ready to spend the bucks, you've had all year to save.

**The Speedway Sparkplugs
Marching Band,
Were so excellent, every year
they stayed in demand.**

The Festival Queen and Princess
take a ride in the corvette,
they were the 500's very best.

Purdue's Marching Band has
the world's largest drum,
It was one of the reasons, why
so many people would come.

Fans cheered loud and proud
for our vets,
They risked their lives, to keep
us safe from threats.

**The Gordon Pipers Bagpipe Band,
Had the coolest sounds in the
entire land.**

Military aircrafts flew over the track,
It was so cool that our soldiers had our back.

Thankful for all who served our beautiful country of America,
We cheered and saluted those who served with integrity and character.

We heard God Bless America,
now let the race begin,
Fans cheered for their favorite
driver to win.

The race had started, 500 miles to go,
I grabbed my food and drinks and was ready for the show.

The fans cheered for every mile,
They were screaming, excited and
had so many smiles.

The pit crew moved very fast,
So the driver's tires would not
cause a crash.

The tires needed to be changed at a fast pace,
so they could get back to the race.

**Drivers are ready for the final lap,
They drove so many miles on the track.**

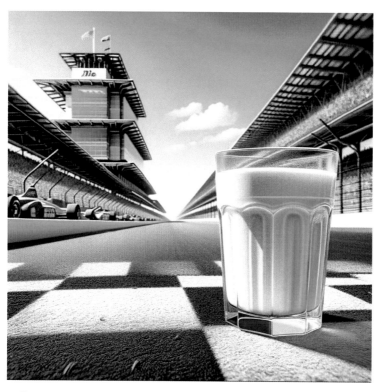

The milk was ready to be consumed by the winner, You've had an amazing race, if that's what you are drinking for dinner.

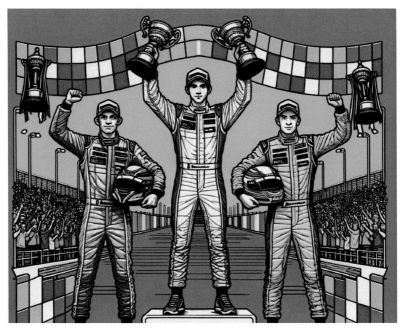

The top 3 finishers stood at the podium to claim their prize, They all felt like champs for their drive.

Fans driving home were thankful for the experience, they can't for next May to cheer again.

Fans had an amazing time as they laughed and cheered, They are already talking about, how they can't wait for next year.

Made in United States
Orlando, FL
04 December 2024

54968928R00015